Met on a Thread

Marisol Murano

Met on a Thread

FICTION / Romance / Contemporary

Paperback ISBN: 978-0-9987510-4-7

www.HipsoMedia.com

CONTENTS

CHAPTER 1

Cotton Dust and Digital Connections

Julia Raven believed in the soul of buildings. In her decade as an architect, she had come to recognize that structures, like people, carried histories in their bones, quiet narratives etched into every beam and brick. Her fingertips traced the cool, weathered surface of the 1851 cotton warehouse she was tasked with transforming, feeling for its secrets. The air in the cavernous space was stale and held a faint memory of cotton dust. Above her, the timber beams of the second floor creaked, a low groaning that was as much a part of its identity as its sturdy brick shell. This building, with its soaring ceilings and the smell of damp earth rising from its foundation, spoke to her.

"You can't possibly finish the proposal by Thursday," came Eliza's voice. "Parker's being unreasonable, as usual."

Julia turned to find her colleague and closest friend, Eliza Wheeler, surveying the vast interior from a sturdy beam that spanned the width of the old warehouse. Eliza, with her wild, rebellious curls forever escaping the confines of her professional bun, was an adventuress who'd bungee jump over the weekend, then calmly present a complex structural analysis come Monday.

Eliza had been the first to welcome Julia when she joined Coastal Heritage Architecture three years ago and remained her strongest ally in the predominantly male firm. Julia, in her dark jeans, work boots, and a well-worn field jacket, was the anchor between them.

"It's a stretch. I agree," Julia said, snapping another photo that detailed the original crown molding, now layered with decades of dust. "But this building deserves someone who'll fight for it."

Eliza rolled her eyes. "So romantic about these old piles of bricks. By the way, are you coming to Theo's gallery opening tonight? His *very single* brother will be there."

"Deadline, remember?" Julia tucked a strand of auburn hair behind her ear, relieved to have a legitimate excuse. Eliza's matchmaking efforts, while well-intentioned, led to awkward evenings with men who looked at her blankly when she talked about sustainable retrofitting or the poetry of negative space.

Back at her apartment—the second floor of a Victorian home in Savannah's historic district—Julia spotted a small plate as she approached the door. She picked up the note that lay on top: "Thought you might need something sweet, darling. The dentist on the first floor asked about you again." Julia smiled. The note was from Mrs. Mercer, her neighbor and landlady. A true Southern matriarch, her heart was as warm as the slice of peach cobbler on the plate.

There was no escaping it. Between Mrs. Mercer and Eliza, it seemed everyone was determined to put an end to Julia's single status, as if being single were something terminal. Julia appreciated their concern, but at thirty-two, she had grown comfortable with her own company, her small circle of friends, and her absorption in her work. Dating had become a distant priority, especially after the spectacular implosion of her engagement two years earlier.

Julia sat on the well-worn couch, kicked off her boots and let out a sigh of relief. She loved this time of day. As she massaged the soles of her aching feet, the chorus of crickets began to swell outside, a steady, rhythmic chirping that was as much a part of Savannah's evening soundtrack as the rustle of palmetto fronds. It was a familiar sound, a comforting, omnipresent hum that soothed the day's strains and settled the scattered thoughts in her mind.

After a while, Julia got up to pour herself a glass of cabernet sauvignon—nothing fancy, just a reliable $18 bottle—and settled at her desk, where architectural drawings and material samples competed for space with her laptop. She opened the Parker proposal file, but found her attention wandering after twenty minutes of budget calculations.

Out of habit, she opened Reddit on her browser. Julia had discovered r/WineEnthusiasts six months ago while researching wine storage options for a client's renovation. What began as professional research had evolved into something of a nightly ritual. She enjoyed the community's mix of novices and experts and the way people shared their discoveries. What she liked best was the anonymity of it all.

Tonight, the top post was from someone seeking recommendations for wines to serve at a summer wedding. Julia scrolled past, looking for something more interesting. Three posts down, she found it:

> **OakBarrelRoller**: *Just inherited my aunt's wine collection. About 50 bottles, mostly French reds from the '90s. Not sure what's worth keeping vs. drinking soon. Any advice on how to filter through this? Storage has been good—temperature-controlled basement in New Hampshire.*

She paused, remembering the small collection her grandmother had left her. Julia had faced a similar dilemma, ultimately keeping three bottles and sharing the rest with family. She began typing:

> **HaintBlueJulia**: *I was in a similar situation with my grandmother's collection. First, document everything (take photos of labels, note fill levels and cork condition). Check*

online auction sites for similar vintages to determine value. Most importantly, decide what matters more to you— monetary value or the experience of tasting a piece of your aunt's life. I kept a few special bottles and opened the rest with people who knew my grandmother. Each bottle turned into a night of stories about her. No regrets.

She hit "post" and returned to her proposal work. An hour later, she checked for responses and found several people had upvoted her comment. One reply caught her eye:

CabernetCrusader: *Great approach to inherited wines. Sharing bottles with people who knew the collector transforms the wine. I helped my uncle catalog his collection.*

Julia clicked on the username. CabernetCrusader's recent posts revealed someone knowledgeable yet without pretense. He responded to beginners' questions with patience and subtly deflected the occasional wine snob. His comments, she noticed, were as much about the connection—to history, to culture—as they were about the wines.

She tried not to overthink her reply. After her breakup with Aaron, Julia had become an overthinker, analyzing every move, every word. It was paralyzing, sometimes.

She typed a response:

HaintBlueJulia: *Any treasures in the collection worth mentioning?*

She closed her laptop and returned to her proposal work, not expecting a response right away. When she checked Reddit before bed, there it was:

CabernetCrusader: *A 1920 Txakoli tucked away in a dusty cellar. It was practically fossilized, covered in cobwebs — more treasure than juice. Too bad the bottle wasn't drinkable. Dust is in my line of work, though.*

HaintBlueJulia: *I know what you mean. I'm an architect. I spend a lot of time sifting through the dust of ages.*

CabernetCrusader: *Sifting through the dust of ages … in search of?*

Julia felt her pulse racing. She responded:

HaintBlueJulia: *Whatever I can save. Currently restoring an 1851 cotton warehouse in Savannah. Spent today documenting wear patterns on brick thresholds. You?*

CabernetCrusader: *Antiques. Step into my shop. That tarnished watch you see? It counted frantic seconds, ticking down to a rendezvous at the old clock tower.*

HaintBlueJulia: *What kind of antiques?*

She hesitated before sending. Her question had nothing to do with wine. But something about CabernetCrusader's responses made the exchange feel natural. She hit "post" and got ready for bed. As she slipped under the covers, her phone chimed with a Reddit notification:

CabernetCrusader: *American furniture and decorative*

objects, primarily 18th and 19th century. My shop in Providence specializes in items with documented histories. When you've finished breathing life back into that cotton warehouse, do share the 'before' and 'after' photos.

Providence. Now she had a location to go with the username. She typed a response:

HaintBlueJulia: *I'll post photos when it's done (another ten months at least). Providence has some beautiful industrial architecture. I'm in Savannah. We're practically architectural opposites—your city built in stone against cold, ours in wood to catch every possible breeze.*

She sent the message and set her alarm, aware she was procrastinating on sleep. As she turned out the light, Julia realized she'd lost an hour chatting with a stranger on Reddit instead of working on her proposal or answering texts from real friends. Yet somehow, the exchange had left her feeling energized.

In Providence, though she couldn't know it, Dylan Gilbert was having similar thoughts as he closed his laptop and glanced at the 18th-century clock ticking steadily on his mantel, marking time as it had for centuries.

CHAPTER 2

The Black Tulip

Dylan Gilbert woke to the familiar creaking of his apartment's wooden floors. The second story of a Federal-style building in Providence's College Hill neighborhood, it sat directly above The Black Tulip, the antique shop he had inherited from his uncle after his mysterious death in search of a rare treasure. Every morning, the floorboard by his bed announced the day with a groan that had likely been there since Thomas Jefferson was president.

He'd fallen asleep with his laptop open again. A quick glance showed three new Reddit notifications—all replies to his comments on r/WineEnthusiasts. The one from HaintBlueJulia was the first he opened.

> *HaintBlueJulia: I'll post photos when it's done (another ten months at least). Providence has some beautiful industrial architecture. I'm in Savannah. We're practically architectural opposites—your city built in stone against cold, ours in wood to catch every possible breeze.*

Dylan smiled. He'd spent far too long last night researching her cotton warehouse project after their exchange. Her perspective on historical preservation resonated with him—seeing buildings as stories, rather than just structures.

CabernetCrusader: *Never been to Savannah. My shop is in this 1803 building that's seen more drama than an Italian opera—everything from a silversmith to a printing press. The walls practically gossip if you listen closely. What hooked you on architectural preservation? Did you rescue a crumbling gargoyle in your youth?*

He hit send before heading downstairs to open the shop. On his way out, he passed a heavy door with original brass hardware; the oak door separated his private space from his public one. The Black Tulip occupied the first floor and basement of the building. It was filled with carefully curated American antiques, each with documented provenance. Unlike some dealers who chased only the highest-value items, Dylan favored pieces that told stories of everyday American life through the centuries.

His assistant, Nico, was waiting outside, coffee in hand.

"Morning, boss," he said, handing over a cup from their favorite local roaster.

"Thanks, Nico. We've got that estate evaluation in Brookline at eleven," Dylan reminded him, unlocking the shop. "The family claims they have a Chippendale secretary. But from the photos, I'm a little skeptical."

Nico had looked at the photos, too. Popular in the 18th century, the Chippendale combined the functional design of a secretary desk with the distinctive stylistic elements of Chippendale furniture—Mahogany wood, graceful S-shaped legs and intricate carvings. They were sought-after antiques, highly elegant and often imposing. But there were many reproductions on the market.

"Bet you twenty bucks it's a reproduction," Nico said, entering the shop.

"I'll pass on that bet," Dylan laughed. "Still worth looking at, though. And who knows, there's always the chance of a hidden compartment … perhaps a forgotten stash of letters. Even in disappointing collections, there's usually something interesting."

As they prepared the shop for opening, Dylan found himself checking his phone more frequently than usual. By mid-morning, a response appeared:

HaintBlueJulia: *I grew up in a new development where every house looked identical. I was only 16 when I visited Charleston. The worn brick and wrought-iron gates were so different. But the haint blue porch ceilings meant to ward off spirits won me over! The Black Tulip sounds intriguing. How did you get the name?*

Dylan waited until his lunch break to reply, wanting to give her question some thought. The past few months had been consumed with settling his uncle's affairs and learning the intricacies of running the business alone. Apart from all the responsibility, Dylan was processing a grief that still caught him off guard at unexpected moments. He kept his reply short.

> **CabernetCrusader:** *'The Black Tulip' is a novel by Alexandre Dumas—about the obsession with rare things. Just curious: Ever face community resistance to your modernization efforts?*

Throughout the afternoon, Dylan kept looking at his phone between customers. The Brookline estate had indeed featured a Colonial Revival reproduction, but Nico had discovered a collection of handwritten recipe books dating back to the 1850s that proved far more interesting. As they drove back to Providence, Dylan received another notification:

> **HaintBlueJulia:** *How did you guess? Current project has a neighborhood group convinced I'm destroying history. Dumas reference noted—I'll have to read it! Do you read much historical fiction?*

Dylan waited until after closing to reply. He sat at his desk surrounded by auction catalogs and condition reports.

> **CabernetCrusader:** *Historical fiction is my guilty pleasure. Currently reading a novel about the Portuguese court's escape to Brazil during the Napoleonic Wars. What are you reading?*

Once the customers left, Dylan finally checked his phone. Three new notifications from the wine forum.

While looking for HaintBlueJulia's reply to his question, he caught sight of a response from another user:

CabernetConnoisseur: *This is a fascinating discussion. But maybe you two should take it to DMs? Rest of us are here for wine recommendations, not architectural philosophy.* 😏

Dylan's stomach tightened. The suggestion was reasonable—their conversation had strayed far from wine—but moving to direct messages meant crossing a line he wasn't ready to cross.

He typed and deleted several responses before settling on:

CabernetCrusader: *So noted! Has anyone tried the new releases from Willamette Valley this season? I'm curious about the 2023 vintage reports.*

Julia stared at her phone. She reread CabernetCrusader's deflection. After a week of increasingly personal exchanges, his sudden retreat felt jarring. Had she misread their connection?

She scrolled back through their conversation thread, analyzing each exchange for signs she'd overstepped. Their discussion had felt natural, intellectually stimulating in a way she hadn't experienced since—well, since Aaron. The thought made her chest tighten with familiar wariness.

Maybe this was for the best. She'd gotten carried away, investing emotional energy in someone she knew only through carefully crafted Reddit comments. She didn't even know his name.

Still, why did she feel so disappointed?

Julia typed a neutral response about Oregon wine regions, then closed the app without posting it. If he wanted to keep his distance, she could respect that boundary. She had her own reasons for proceeding carefully.

Over the next couple of days, their interactions remained strictly wine-focused. Dylan answered her questions about vintage recommendations with short, polite answers. Julia shared tasting notes from a local wine bar without mentioning the architectural details of the restored 1920s building that housed it. Both carefully avoided the personal tangents that had marked their earlier exchanges.

Dylan told himself this was for the better. Yet he found himself checking the forum more frequently, hoping for glimpses of HaintBlueJulia's wit. Despite his determination to keep his distance, her posts intrigued him. It was in the forum that he learned she'd spent a summer in Italy. He loved Italian wines. Italy was on his bucket list. Above all, he wanted to continue their conversation.

CabernetCrusader: *Was a summer in Italy long enough to sample the wines?*

HaintBlueJulia: *Short enough to spark curiosity. Long enough to cover the subject.*

Dylan smiled. But he was not sure what to respond.

They were caught in an uncomfortable middle ground—too invested to ignore each other completely, too wary to risk getting closer. Dylan composed more personal responses, then edited them back to safe wine recommendations. Julia drafted questions about his work, then deleted them in favor of queries about wine storage.

The wine forum had become both a bridge and a barrier—keeping them in touch, while preventing the intimacy that had begun to develop.

By the end of the week, Julia felt beaten down. Deadlines shifted like sand dunes, a critical structural report was delayed, and Parker, her boss, had perfected the art of the passive-aggressive email. By Friday afternoon, all Julia wanted was to get out of her work clothes, curl up with a book, and pretend her job didn't require her to analyze the tensile strength of historic mortar. The thought of spending another Friday night alone, watching the hum of the Savannah streetlights from her window, felt particularly discouraging.

Determined to salvage at least one part of her week, she left work a little earlier than usual and headed to the flower market.

At home, she changed into a sundress and went to see Mrs. Mercer. The afternoon was humid; the giant oaks looked languid, hanging low. She reached Mrs. Mercer's front door just as a familiar figure was coming up the porch steps. It was Dr. Da Silva, the dentist who occupied the first floor of their Victorian home. A true extrovert, Dr. Da Silva was a man who spoke in tangents and surveyed the world looking for listeners. That afternoon, he wore a Hawaiian shirt patterned with miniature pineapples, over white linen pants. He looked like he'd just stepped off a cruise ship.

"Dr. Da Silva?" Julia blinked, holding a bouquet of freshly cut, fragrant gardenias. She meant to thank Mrs. Mercer for the peach cobbler, and so much more. Dr. Da Silva smiled, a bright smile you'd expect from someone in his line of work. His light green eyes were animated behind rimless glasses that had started to cloud.

"Julia, darling! What a coincidence! But is anything truly a coincidence when the universe conspires to bring good intentions together? As I was just telling my hygienist, Mildred, a smile is a powerful thing. It's not just about the pearly whites …" As Dr. Da Silva went on, Julia's gaze drifted to the small, potted orchid in his hands. The door swung open. It was Mrs. Mercer, a vision in soft lavender. Her silver hair was perfectly coiffed, and nothing in her manner indicated the nearly suffocating heat of the afternoon.

"Why, Dr. Da Silva, Julia, darlings!" she said, in her melodious drawl. "What a delightful surprise, and with such beautiful offerings!" Her deep eyes twinkled. "Come in. Come in."

Dr. Da Silva puffed out his chest. "A gift for you, Mrs. Mercer! A small token of my appreciation for your kindness. And, of course, for your generosity with the... rent reprieve."

"Oh, you two are just too sweet," Mrs. Mercer cooed. "I was just about to make a fresh pitcher of lemonade."

They stepped into Mrs. Mercer's parlor, a room as warm as a hug. Sunlight streamed through tall, lace-curtained windows, illuminating dust motes dancing in the air. A floral sofa in a faded chintz dominated one wall, flanked by two mahogany armchairs.

Mrs. Mercer gestured to the armchairs. "Please, make yourselves comfortable." Dr. Da Silva immediately gravitated to one, while Julia, trying to maintain a polite distance, went toward the other.

"So, Julia," Dr. Da Silva began. "Busy week, eh? Tore any buildings down today?"

Julia managed a thin smile, her eyes darting to Mrs. Mercer in the kitchen. "Yes. Preservation work, mostly."

"Ah, preservation!" he said. "It's like crowns, I suppose. He chuckled loudly at his own joke.

"Let me help you with the glasses," Julia said to Mrs. Mercer. She poured the lemonade, then took a sip. "This is so refreshing. My grandmother made it exactly—down to the mint leaves!"

Mrs. Mercer smiled at Julia and interjected smoothly, "Oh, Dr. Da Silva, you must tell me again about that marvelous new hygienist you hired. Mildred, wasn't it?"

At this, Dr. Da Silva launched into a new monologue about Mildred's exceptional dental technique. Julia nodded along, feigning interest. After a while, she excused herself with a mention of early morning plans. Mrs. Mercer took the cue and walked her to the door while Dr. Da Silva's monologue continued, undeterred by Julia's departure.

"Such a busy girl you are. Thank you for this lovely visit," she said, patting her hand. "And the gardenias!" Busy, yes. But perhaps, also a little lonely. Julia felt a pang of disappointment. It had something to do with the sadness Mrs. Mercer had guessed in her.

When she entered her apartment, the long weekend stretched in front of her. She was hungry. Her hair needed washing. She opened her computer and clicked on her usual online haunts, including the wine forum. Nothing new or exciting had been posted. She stopped typing and looked at her chipped fingernails. All of a sudden, she felt that all of her was broken. She headed for the freezer, grabbed a pint of raspberry sorbet and returned to the couch. What was CabernetCrusader doing on a Friday night? She wondered. The thought struck her as ridiculous. It had been a long draining week. She just needed some rest.

Their online standoff might have continued indefinitely, if not for a single post that would change everything between them.

CHAPTER 3

Direct Messages

On Sunday morning, Julia woke up, made a pot of coffee and posted about discovering a bottle of 1967 Château d'Yquem while cleaning out her grandmother's house:

HaintBlueJulia: *Found this treasure hiding behind mason jars of peach preserves. Label is pristine. Fill level looks good. Worth saving for a special occasion. She saved it for 50+ years—not sure she ever found an occasion special enough.*

Dylan read the post three times. Possibly the greatest sweet wine in the world, Château d'Yquem was known for its incredible complexity, longevity, and balance. There were numerous legendary vintages, but few rivaled the reputation of the 1967 for its luscious sweetness and the vibrant acidity that allowed it to age well over decades. It was a lucky find. Dylan was excited, just reading about it.

Before he could second-guess himself, he typed:

CabernetCrusader: *That vintage is extraordinary—*

honeyed, complex, with notes that unfold for hours. But wine isn't meant to be preserved indefinitely. The special occasion isn't what warrants the wine. Sometimes, the wine makes the occasion special.

His response was more personal than anything he'd written in a while. Dylan hesitated before posting, aware he was revealing too much about his current state of mind. Everything he knew about wine, he owed to Uncle Tobias. His late uncle, who loved life and wine in equal measure, and who often said that uncorking a young Bordeaux was to commit infanticide with a corkscrew, what would he say about HaintBlueJulia and her treasure? He'd probably advise to wait for a spectacular occasion, worthy of this wine. But after what happened in Turkey, Dylan wasn't so sure. Was there an occasion in life big enough for a bottle like this? He meant what he had said to HaintBlueJulia. But he didn't want to get too personal in an online forum crowded with strangers.

Julia read his comment, surprised by the recognition. Here was someone who understood the cost of perpetual postponement. Someone who, like her, might be holding back.

She typed a more personal response, too:

HaintBlueJulia: *You have a point. Anticipation can become its own trap. I think Grandma was saving the bottle for a mythical "perfect moment" that never came. Maybe the lesson isn't about finding the right occasion. Is a bag of tortilla* *chips special enough?*

CabernetCrusader: *A bag of tortilla chips? Well, it depends on the chips. Are we talking artisanal, small-batch, heirloom corn chips with a story? Or the kind you find at a gas station, destined for immediate, unapologetic crunching? Must confess, I was picturing something a little more ... candlelit.*

HaintBlueJulia: *Oh, a purist, are you? Candlelight can be arranged. Intrigue, too. You can always start with the Yquem and then ... improvise? If only we were bold enough to give this bottle a fair shake.*

Dylan stopped, a thoughtful pause, then a smile you could almost hear.

CabernetCrusader: *A fair shake. Now, that's an intriguing proposition – to let the wine guide the evening. It's a kind of defiance against the tyranny of the 'perfect' occasion. And perhaps the wine will feel less judged.*

HaintBlueJulia: *Precisely! No pressure for it to be a Nobel Prize ceremony. Just two people, a legendary bottle, and the courage to make an ordinary night unforgettable.*

Dylan stared at her reply. It was more of a challenge. Her post challenged him to think beyond his own carefully-curated world. He liked the controlled connection they had, a friendship without the complications of deeper involvement. The complexity of a new relationship—even a digital one—felt like more than he could handle at this point. But it also bothered him that their public exchanges were drawing attention from other members. Several had commented on their lengthy discussions, some with amusement, others with mild irritation.

Before he could change his mind, he typed:

CabernetCrusader: *I think we're in agreement. No need to wait for world peace, or a comet strike! The best kind of special occasion might be the one you create. And besides, that bottle has waited long enough. Should we take this conversation private?*

After a few minutes of internal debate, Dylan composed a sort of disclaimer. The disclaimer felt necessary—a gentle way to set expectations.

CabernetCrusader: *Fair warning. It may take me a while to respond. Too much to explain here. I've genuinely enjoyed our exchanges, though.*

Julia's stomach did a flip-flop. Fair warning. Given her own wariness about rushing into things, his caution was reassuring. Sort of.

She waited until early Sunday afternoon to send him the first direct message:

Dylan was in his workshop, an airy space just outside Newport, when his phone buzzed.

Julia: *Hello there.*

Dylan: *Hello back.*

He was sanding a cedar plank, the rhythmic rasp of sandpaper against the quiet hum of the ventilation fan. He stopped and flexed his hands, the muscles in his forearms sharp from years of wrestling with stubborn timber.

Julia: *Thank you for the fair warning. And for taking this little tangent off the main road.*

Julia was curled on her window seat, avoiding doing laundry. A heap of clothes threatened to take over her reading nook.

Dylan: *What else is there to talk about, besides wine?*

Julia: *(typing...)*

Dylan: *Just kidding! What does a professional building whisperer do on a Sunday?*

Julia: *Sundays mostly involve coffee. And avoiding laundry. Do you have a laundry avoidance mechanism?*

Dylan: *Good question. Restoring old wooden boats is my Sunday pastime.*

Julia: *Old wooden boats? Sounds tactile … And meditative.*

Dylan: *Would you say you're a procrastinator in general, or is the laundry your main target for avoidance?*

Julia: *Very good question. Back at you. Avoiding anything in particular?*

Dylan paused. He thought about the unopened mail on his desk, and everything else he'd been postponing. He picked up a piece of sandpaper, rubbing it against the cedar.

Dylan: *A thorny truth, perhaps.*

Julia: *Thorny?*

Dylan: *Let's say I'm in the middle of a long goodbye.*

Julia: *Ah, one of those …*

Dylan: *(He let out a short breath). It's a tricky situation. You? What kind of things are you avoiding?*

Julia: *Me? The usual: sugar, professional backstabbers, boring dates, anything that reads 'one size fits all,' rogue hair ties that leave for another dimension when you need them most, dating apps, flat-pack furniture with missing parts. Let's see … what else?*

Dylan: *Is that all? My mom's Sunday texts are beginning to look reasonable.*

Julia: *Ah yes. Mothers tend to have the last word, don't they?*

Dylan: *Not my mother. She has the first word, the last word and every word in between. Speaking of which, I'd better check in. Thanks for the chat, Julia.*

Julia: *Anytime.*

Dylan: *Talk soon.*

Over the next several days, Dylan found himself reaching for his phone first thing each morning and checking for messages throughout the day. Still, he remained guarded about anything too personal.

Julia was no expert at chitchat, either. Socializing and making small talk required a type of energy she had never had.

During their chats, Dylan learned that Julia had grown up in Atlanta before moving to Savannah for work and that she had a younger brother in California. She told him a little more about that summer she spent in Italy, documenting Renaissance buildings. From him she learned he was an only child, about his Massachusetts childhood, and his passion for restoring old wooden boats.

One evening after work, Dylan sat cross legged on the floor eating leftover pizza. He wondered what it would be like to see the space where Julia lived, to watch her work on her designs, to share a glass of wine. The thought surprised him. He decided to text her.

Dylan: *So, where do you hang your hard hat after a long day of brick whispering? Somewhere with good bones would be my guess.*

Julia: *Victorian bones with modern comfort. Original heart pine floors and crown molding, but contemporary furniture and way too many architectural books and material samples. My dining table is currently hosting three different types of sustainable insulation options. Not exactly House Beautiful material. And you? Is your space perfectly curated, like a museum, or do you cherish the chaos of uncatalogued treasures?*

Dylan: *Hardly. My apartment looks like a library that was barely missed by a meteor. The shop is meticulously organized* *because it's my professional space.*

Their conversations gradually deepened. Dylan shared stories about unusual items that came through his shop—a Civil War surgeon's kit complete with bone saw and a tea service that had supposedly belonged to Abigail Adams. Julia described the excitement of uncovering original architectural elements, and the frustration of working with historical commissions more concerned with regulation than preservation.

They discovered shared interests in jazz and travel photography. Dylan mentioned his goal of visiting every lighthouse in New England.

The more they shared, the more Dylan's initial wariness began to soften, but up to a point. Julia respected his measured pace. It often took him a day or two to respond. Still, he remained guarded. This made Julia wonder if he was hiding anything. When she asked about what had drawn him to antiques, he spoke about appreciating objects with stories and avoided discussing anything more specific.

Their exchanges had become important to him —a bright spot in days that had turned gray since Uncle Tobias' disappearance. For the first time in months, he looked forward to something beyond work obligations and his futile search for an explanation that made sense.

One evening, as Dylan was closing the shop, his phone chimed with a message he was not ready to receive:

Julia: *This might be premature, but I've been invited to* *present at a sustainable preservation conference in Boston next month. Providence isn't far from there, is it? Would be interesting to meet in person. No pressure at all—just thought I'd mention it.*

Dylan read the message, his heart suddenly racing. Meeting in person would turn their digital connection into something real—with all the possibilities and complications that entailed; the careful boundaries he'd established would become meaningless.

Yet, the idea of meeting Julia in person excited him. After weeks of wondering about the person behind the messages, the opportunity to meet her felt like the right thing.

He read her message again, aware of how carefully she'd framed the invitation—mentioning her professional reason for being in Boston, emphasizing the geographical convenience, offering him the freedom to decline.

Dylan looked around The Black Tulip's interior, filled with objects that had survived centuries. Everything was still and settled. And this filled him with peace. Was he ready to take a chance, to move his life in a different direction? He wasn't sure. HaintBlueJulia at the wine forum had taken him completely by surprise.

He began typing a response, then stopped, then started again. The decision felt monumental—not just about meeting Julia, but about whether he was ready to leave the safety of the life he had built around objects and step into a future that suddenly felt very much alive.

He slid the phone in his pocket. He would have to think about this. It was a harmless invitation, potentially joyful. What was he afraid of?

CHAPTER 4

Searching for Truth

Julia and Eliza were reviewing material samples for the cotton warehouse project, but Julia had been checking her phone for the past five minutes.

"You're chatting with him again?" Eliza said.

"Sorry," Julia said, setting her phone down and refocusing on the pine flooring samples spread across her desk. She took in Eliza's emerald green fingernails and the asymmetrical shirt with a cinched bow at the waist and smiled. If Eliza stood for anything, it was for the freedom to be comfortable in your own skin. Julia loved this quality in her friend.

"I'm starting to worry," Eliza said. "I haven't seen you this deep into a guy since . . . well, ever."

Julia felt her cheeks warm. "Dylan and I just have these great conversations about preservation and stuff."

"Dylan? Not CabernetCrusader? Have you been

holding out on me, Julia Raven?" Eliza's eyebrows rose. "I feel I've been led into a dark cave!"

"The drama," Julia said.

Eliza was not wrong. Julia had told her about the online conversations, after they'd moved to direct messages. But in the days since they'd exchanged first names, their conversations had deepened considerably.

"We've been texting," Julia admitted. "Regular texting. It's just easier."

Eliza picked up one of the wood samples. "And my name is Marilyn Monroe."

"Stop!" Julia protested, though not as harshly as she'd intended. "We're just . . . kindred spirits in that regard."

"What regard? The last time I texted anyone as frequently as you've been doing was when I started dating Theo," Eliza said. "Just be careful. Promise?"

Julia nodded, knowing her friend meant well.

Her phone vibrated with a new message, and Julia fought the urge to check it right away.

"Go ahead," Eliza said, smiling. "I need to make a call to the contractor." She grabbed her tablet and left Julia's office.

Julia picked up her phone, seeing Dylan's response to her earlier message about a difficult client meeting:

Dylan: *Maybe you should create a mandatory architectural appreciation course for all your clients.*

She smiled and typed back:

Julia: Clever idea. I'll just add that to the contract: "Client agrees to complete 40 hours of architectural history education before demolishing any original features." Would save me so many arguments!

Dylan: I'm behind this initiative. Speaking of education, I found something you might appreciate—1920s architectural drawings for a Providence textile mill. Previous owner had them framed as art. Beautiful draftsmanship.

He attached a photo of detailed hand-drawn plans, the pencil lines still crisp after nearly a century, the precision of the measurements and annotations reflecting a craftsmanship that had largely disappeared in the digital age.

Julia: Those are stunning. The hand lettering alone is a lost art. Most of my work is digital now, though I still sketch by hand for initial concepts.

Dylan: Letters vs. emails. Even if they both say the same thing, the hands carry more of the sender's ... essence somehow.

In this last message, Julia saw a kind of opening. She wasn't sure how to follow up about Boston. She hesitated before typing her next message:

Julia: Speaking of essence ... We've never actually seen each other.

The moment she hit send, Julia wished she hadn't. Was

she pushing too hard? They had shared thoughts, opinions, and stories for weeks, but had carefully avoided the subject of her invitation. From the start, they had agreed to no photos and no social media connections. It had kept their relationship unpolluted, which felt both safer and more meaningful. But with her Boston conference approaching, she didn't want to miss the chance of meeting Dylan.

Several minutes passed before Dylan responded:

Dylan: *Mystery has its charm, but we should probably be able to recognize each other at some point.*

At some point, Julia said aloud.

Another moment passed, then a photo appeared. Dylan stood beside an antique desk. He had dark, wavy hair and intensely focused eyes. He wore a fitted charcoal t-shirt. His forearms suggested he did more than just sell antiques.

Julia studied the photo longer than necessary, absorbing details. He looked . . . real, like someone captured in his natural habitat, surrounded by the things he loved.

She scrolled through her recent photos, looking for one to share in return. Most were architectural—buildings, details, materials. The few that included her were group shots from work events or selfies with Eliza. Finally, she found one that Eliza had taken a few months ago during a site visit. Julia stood in front of the cotton warehouse in its pre-renovation state, her auburn hair pulled back, wearing jeans and a simple blue button-down shirt.

Julia: *This is me in my natural habitat—at home in a pile of rubble.*

Dylan's response came quickly:

Dylan: *Now I can stop imagining you as an avatar with a haint blue background! You look exactly as I expected—observant and engaged. I feel like I've seen that expression many times before . . .*

Julia smiled at his response, which managed to acknowledge her appearance without making it the focus. Before she could reply, her phone rang—her contractor with questions about the warehouse's electrical system. By the time she finished the call, Eliza had returned, and they spent the rest of the afternoon finalizing material selections.

That evening, sitting on her small balcony with a glass of Portuguese *vinho verde* (chosen partly because Dylan had mentioned enjoying it), Julia returned to their conversation:

Julia: *Sorry for disappearing earlier—more work chaos. How was your day?*

His response came quickly:

Dylan: *Quiet. That Chippendale chair may be over 200 years old, but it's remarkably tight-lipped about the tea it's seen.*

Julia: *I'll trade your tight-lipped chair for my noisy clients any day of the week!*

Their conversation continued, even as Julia prepared dinner (pasta with farmers market vegetables) and afterward as she reviewed project timelines. Around ten, Dylan sent:

Dylan: *I should probably stop monopolizing your evening and get some sleep myself. Early estate auction tomorrow in Newport.*

Julia: *You're not monopolizing—this is the highlight of my day.*

Dylan: *Hosting a wine tasting at the shop next weekend. Educational event for clients, focusing on historic winemaking regions. Wish you could attend.*

Julia smiled.

Julia: *Sounds wonderful. I'd come, if Providence weren't 900 miles away. Boston is a lot closer, though.*

Dylan: *What is it about you?*

Julia: *I don't know what you mean.*

Dylan: *There's one more thing I need to know before agreeing to Boston.*

Julia: *What's that?*

Dylan: *Do you have a middle name?*

Julia: *Celeste.*

Dylan: *I was hoping for that. Good night, Julia Celeste.*

Julia set her phone down, and couldn't help a big,

growing grin. His message had come at 10 p.m. She settled in bed, staring at the screen. She was nervous. She was giddy. She was terrified. Boston. She felt the thrill of finally putting a face to his name, to his voice. Their conversations had become a constant in her daily life—morning check-ins, midday anecdotes, evening discussions that often stretched late into the night. There was something uniquely intimate about what they shared. She felt an overwhelming urge to text him back, to say something more. But she resisted. He had taken her by surprise. He wanted to know more about her. She turned off her lamp and fell asleep to a symphony of crickets.

The next morning Julia woke up and checked her phone. But there was nothing from Dylan. That was strange, especially after their agreement to meet in Boston. She sent him a message:

Julia: *Hello there—how's it going in Newport?*

She tossed her phone onto the bed. The "Do Not Disturb" reply felt like a splash of water. This wasn't like Dylan. She got up from the bed and felt strangely unsettled, a gnawing discomfort that stuck to her as morning light crept into her bedroom.

She looked at her reflection in the bathroom mirror. The excitement from the night before was now replaced by a prickly unease. She washed her face and brushed her teeth. She had to get ready for work. In a little while she was dabbing on foundation, then blush, then mascara; her movements automatic. She pulled on a crisp white button-down, then immediately peeled it off. Next, a softer, flowing silk blouse. She settled on a gray knit top that she actually didn't like, thinking all the while that she had pushed Dylan too far. But what if something had happened to him? This was not like him. But what, exactly, did she know about him to even think that?

The bakery, usually a haven of warmth and the sweet scent of baking, felt different this morning. Julia ordered her usual: a large coffee with cream and sugar, and a blueberry muffin. She sat at a small table by the window and found the light too bright. She felt restless. She grabbed her phone. Still, nothing.

She took a bite of the muffin. The burst of sweet blueberries she loved did little to settle the unease in her stomach. What had happened? A series of rationalizations went through her mind: he forgot his charger, he got swamped, maybe something went wrong at the estate auction—perhaps a rival bidder had turned nasty, or a priceless piece had been damaged. But Dylan wasn't absent-minded. A forgotten charger? That didn't feel right. He'd changed his mind about Boston, she concluded. It was too risky. Too much too soon. Too big a commitment.

Since her breakup with Aaron, trust felt like a bruise that would not heal, an ache that flared at unexpected moments. Julia told herself there was no logical reason she should feel so emptied out, so adrift, just for a few hours of missing texts from someone she'd only known online. This wasn't productive. She sighed, placed the remaining half of the muffin into the paper bag, and headed toward her car with the nagging wonder that something was wrong with her.

The day turned out to be a whirlwind of meetings and back-to-back video calls, each demanding Julia's full attention. She'd navigated a heated debate with a developer and managed to secure a crucial permit just before the city office closed. Yet, beneath the professional calm, her tension mounted. Her phone lay beside her keyboard like a reproach. Around 3 p.m., as the last meeting ended, she finally gave in. She settled on something simple: *"Hey. Hope auctioneer didn't hijack your phone."*

At a quarter till five, Eliza came into Julia's office.

"A few of us are going to Riverview for happy hour. Come?"

Julia looked up from her computer. "I have to review the electrical contractor's proposal tonight."

Eliza gave her a knowing look. "You mean you have plans to text with Dylan, while pretending to review the proposal."

"That's not ..." Julia began, then stopped herself.

"When was the last time you came out with the team? Or went out with anyone you could actually see and touch?"

Julia felt a flash of defensiveness. "That's not fair. You know I've been busy with the warehouse project."

"True. And spending every free minute texting with a man you've never met," Eliza added. "Look, I'm not judging. Just making sure this online thing isn't a way to avoid …"

"We're meeting in three weeks," Julia interrupted.

"And I'm super excited for you," Eliza said. "Just come have one drink with actual three-dimensional humans tonight, okay? You can text him from the bar if you want."

Eliza had a point. She had been declining invitations more frequently lately. She preferred the ease of her text conversations with Dylan. And she always felt exhausted after in-person socializing.

At Riverview, a trendy bar overlooking the Savannah River, Julia found herself actually enjoying the company of her colleagues. She'd forgotten how much she liked the creative energy of their team gatherings, the shop talk that evolved into more personal conversations as the evening progressed.

Quinn, the firm's newest architect, sat next to her during their second round of drinks.

"I've been wanting to ask you about the warehouse project," he said. "Is it true you found original heart pine beams under the drop ceiling?"

The project was gnarly. And his sincere excitement made her feel good about the slow progress. They started talking and she pulled up photos of the beams on her phone to show him the growth rings that indicated old-growth timber, likely harvested in the early 1800s.

"That's incredible," Quinn said, leaning closer to see the photos. "The craftsmanship from that era is just unmatched." As he leaned into her phone, Julia caught a whiff of his cologne. Something fresh that reminded her of walking through a forest.

They talked for a while. Quinn showed her photos of a renovation project he'd worked on in Charleston, their heads bent together over his phone, when she heard Eliza's voice:

"Look at you two—architectural nerds."

Quinn blushed a little, and Julia realized how their position might appear to observers—heads close together, sharing photos.

"Julia's showing me the original beams from the warehouse project," Quinn said, his voice a little tighter than usual.

"And Quinn was just telling me about a hidden fireplace he discovered during a Charleston renovation," Julia added.

Eliza bit her lower lip. "It's cute watching you two geek out. Quinn, fair warning—Julia's heart belongs to a mysterious antique dealer from Providence."

Now it was Julia's turn to blush. "He's a friend in Providence with similar interests," she clarified, seeing

Quinn's eyes looking away.

But Quinn recovered quickly. "Providence? I have a cousin who went to RISD. Great architectural city."

"That's what I've heard," Julia said, grateful for his graceful pivot. "Dylan—my friend—has mentioned some of the historic restoration projects there."

Her phone vibrated, and this time she glanced down to see multiple messages from Dylan:

Dylan: *Right you were! Silence phones for rapid-fire bidding war. Glad I went. How was your day?*

Julia looked at the message and was about to respond when Quinn asked her a question about sustainable insulation options, pulling her back into their conversation.

The evening continued, with Julia torn between being present with her colleagues while glancing at incoming messages from Dylan. By the time they all said goodnight outside the bar, she realized that Eliza had been right—she had needed this real-world social interaction.

Walking to her car, she finally responded to Dylan's texts:

Julia: *Sorry for the delayed response—was out with colleagues. Curious to learn more about your finds.*

His response came as she was unlocking her apartment door:

Dylan: *No apology needed.*

Julia settled onto her sofa, kicking off her shoes and curling her legs beneath her. She had had a little too much to drink and was feeling drowsy.

Just before midnight, she sent:

Julia: *I should get some sleep, but looking forward to photos of your finds at the auction.*

Dylan: *Have a good night.*

Julia set her phone on the nightstand. The prospect of turning their connection into a reality was both thrilling and scary. What if the chemistry they shared through text didn't translate to the physical world? What if the Dylan she had come to know through carefully composed messages was different from the real-life person she would meet in Boston?

Or worse—what if he was exactly as she imagined, but she somehow disappointed him?

Julia pushed these thoughts away as she drifted into sleep. Whatever happened in Boston, their connection had already given her something valuable—a reminder that somewhere out there existed people who shared her way of seeing the world, someone who valued what was withered and weathered as much as she did.

CHAPTER 5

Trust on Trial

Dylan leaned against the counter of The Black Tulip, watching Nico charm a pair of wealthy customers interested in Federal-period silver.

His phone vibrated in his pocket, but the shop was busy and he resisted the urge to check it. Once the customers moved to examine dining chairs, Dylan checked his phone:

Julia: Just arrived at the warehouse. Contractor removed a section of plaster we were planning to preserve. Having a minor preservation crisis. Plz send antique-lover solidarity.

Dylan smiled and replied:

Dylan: Contractor crimes against history! Full solidarity from the antique trenches. Can the plaster be restored, or is it a total loss?

"The Carmichaels are ready to purchase the teapot and chairs," Nico said, interrupting Dylan's typing. "Judging by your expression, you're texting Savannah."

Dylan shook his head and pocketed his phone. As Cecilia Barnes, a highly sought-after interior designer in Providence, sat down to discuss options for a client's home, she said, "Nico tells me you're meeting someone special soon."

Dylan shot a look at Nico, who was pretending to dust a bookcase nearby. "As you know . . . Nico has an overactive imagination."

"Don't blame the messenger," Nico chimed in.

Cecilia leaned forward. "It's nice to see you interested in something besides furniture, Dylan. I know how hard the past several months have been. God knows how much I miss Tobias!"

Dylan shifted uncomfortably in his chair. He picked up one of the catalogs from his desk and looked at Cecilia. She was perched casually on the edge of his desk, her rhinestone glasses twinkling in the light.

"She's an architect specializing in historical preservation," he said, a little too quickly. "We have some things in common. That's all."

"Oooh, I see some possibility," she said, smiling.

"Should we go over these?" Dylan said, clearing his throat. "We have a lot of ground to cover."

"That we do," she agreed, sliding gracefully off the desk and taking off her rhinestone glasses with a flourish, letting them dangle from one hand. "You know, Dylan. Ghosts are infinitely patient. They're happy to sit around in their swimming trunks until they get your attention."

He looked at her for a beat, then his eyes started darting around the room. "That's, that's . . . good to know. I'll have to keep that in mind."

He swallowed hard and grabbed the top catalog.

"Forget the catalog, dear. I'm thinking three Buddhas from the Angkor Empire for a wide wall in a great room."

"But Cecilia . . ."

"With documented histories, of course. My client has resources."

"Of course."

After Cecilia left, Dylan checked his phone:

Julia: Plaster crisis averted. How's your day?

Dylan: A little trickier than expected.

Julia: Oh? Is it a top-secret kind of tricky?

It wasn't like Dylan not to respond. This gave Julia some pause.

Later that evening, as Julia sat on her sofa with a glass of wine, her phone chimed with an incoming call. Her brother's name flashed on the screen.

"Hey, James," she said, tucking her feet beneath her.

"Hey, sis."

"What are you up to?"

"Nothing much. The reason I'm calling … Listen, mom mentioned you're meeting some guy from Reddit in

Boston."

Julia sighed. She should have known their mother would not keep a confidence. "His name is Dylan," she said. "He owns an antique shop in Providence. We connected through a wine forum on Reddit."

"A Reddit romance," James said. But his tone was serious. "Julia, have you actually verified any of this? The shop? His identity?"

"We've exchanged photos, talked on the phone—"

"You know that's not what I'm asking," James interrupted. "After what happened with Aaron, I figured you'd be more cautious."

The mention of her ex-fiancé sent a pang through Julia. She set the wine glass on the side table. Eighteen months had passed since she'd discovered Aaron wasn't the successful architect he'd claimed to be, but a draftsman who'd stolen project photos from his employer and fabricated an entire career. By the time she uncovered the truth, Julia and Aaron had been living together and had grown a circle of mutual friends. His betrayal had left deep scars.

"This is different," Julia said. But her voice lacked conviction. "Dylan and I talk about substantive things— architecture, history, preservation. It's not like he's trying to impress me with fake credentials."

"I can't be the judge of that. Still, people can be passionate about a lot of things without being who they claim to be. Have you Googled him? The shop?"

"We'd set some ground rules," Julia admitted. But her discomfort was growing. "We just . . . didn't want to ruin a good thing, James."

"Julia," her brother's voice softened. "I'm not trying to rain on your parade. But please do some basic checking before meeting this guy. True or false information won't change what you've shared. It will just help you make an informed decision. And maybe save you some heartache."

After they hung up, Julia stared at her wine glass and started to think about what her brother had said. James had a point. Plus, there was no forgetting the hand grenade Aaron had lobbed at her heart. Julia had researched countless buildings, materials, and architectural firms, yet had shied away from doing the most basic search on someone she was planning to meet. She could have at least googled The Black Tulip.

After some soul searching, she didn't like the answer she got as to why she had not: fear. Fear that Dylan might not be real, that their connection might be built on lies, that she'd been fooled again.

Julia got her laptop and opened a browser. Her fingers trembled a little as she typed: "The Black Tulip antique shop, Providence."

She hit enter and waited, heart racing.

No results matched her search.

She tried again, adding variations: "Black Tulip Rhode

Island antiques," "Dylan Gilbert antiques Providence," "The Black Tulip College Hill."

Nothing. No website, no business listings, no social media pages. Not even a mention in Providence business directories or tourist recommendations.

"This doesn't make sense," Julia said aloud, switching to Google Maps and searching for The Black Tulip near the College Hill neighborhood Dylan had mentioned.

No results.

She tried searching for antique shops in Providence, scanning the list for anything that might be his shop under a different name. Several appeared, but none in the location he'd described, none with names remotely similar.

All of a sudden, she felt queasy. She searched property records for Providence, looking for Dylan Gilbert as a business owner or property holder.

Nothing.

She switched tactics, searching architectural archives and historic building databases for the address he'd mentioned—an 1803 Federal building that had originally housed a silversmith. She found several buildings from that period in Providence but couldn't connect any to Dylan's descriptions without a specific address.

As an architect, Julia knew dozens of ways to verify buildings and businesses. She'd tracked down obscure historical structures with minimal information countless times. Yet every avenue she tried led nowhere, except for:

The Black Tulip, a novel by Alexandre Dumas.

After two hours of disheartening searching, Julia sat back, her earlier warmth from the wine replaced by a chill. The Black Tulip didn't exist—at least not in any verifiable way. And if the shop was fictional, what about its owner?

Her phone chimed with a message:

Dylan: *Just closed up the shop. Rare find today: a Federal-period desk with a hidden compartment—the craftsmanship is exquisite. Made me think of your warehouse project ... How was your day?*

Julia stared at the message, her finger hovering over the screen. The words sounded like Dylan—thoughtful, connecting their interests, asking about her day. But was there actually a shop to close? A desk to discover? Or was it all made up?

She set the phone down without responding, her mind racing. Had she fabricated their entire connection based on carefully crafted messages from a stranger? Was she about to be humiliated again?

Something didn't add up. Their conversations had been consistent, detailed, knowledgeable. If Dylan had made up a fictional persona, why choose an antique dealer? Why not something more impressive or lucrative? And besides, he knew his wines. But then, Julia thought about what James had said about that. A mass murderer could have a thing for vintage Claret.

Julia's phone chimed again:

Dylan: *Hope I didn't interrupt something important. Just wanted to say I'm looking forward to Boston.*

She felt tears pricking at her eyes. The message seemed so normal, so much like the dozens they'd exchanged. How could she reconcile these thoughtful texts with the absence of evidence for The Black Tulip?

Tomorrow, she would have to decide—confront him directly, continue searching for information, or walk away from whatever this was before getting more invested. But tonight, the certainties she'd felt about their connection had been replaced by the ghosts of her past and familiar warnings about trust.

As Julia got ready for bed, her hand hovered over her phone. She was about to respond but stopped herself. Instead, she turned the phone face-down on her nightstand. She would not text another word until she figured out exactly *who* was on the other end.

CHAPTER 6

Ghosting

Julia stared at the small screen. Another message from Dylan:

Dylan: *Are you okay? Not like you to go silent. Did I say something to upset you?*

It was his third message since she'd stopped responding. Each one increased the unease sensation in her stomach.

The morning light filtering through the window was bright. Julia's laptop was still open on the table, alongside scattered notes of addresses and business listings she'd searched. She'd spent hours combing through every possible record of The Black Tulip's existence. Nothing had turned up.

Her phone chimed again:

Dylan: *Julia, I'm starting to worry. Please just let me know you're okay.*

She picked up her phone and began typing:

I've been trying to find information about The Black Tulip online and can't find any evidence it exists. No website, no business listings, nothing. I need to understand why.

She stared at the message, then deleted it without sending. Too accusatory.

She tried again:

Before we meet in Boston, I should probably know more about your shop. When I searched, I couldn't find any online presence for The Black Tulip. Can you explain?

Better, but still off. She set the phone down and walked to the kitchen to make coffee. She rubbed her temples while the coffee brewed. She felt a headache coming on.

Even after all this time, it was hard to forget the humiliation Julia had felt after discovering Aaron's lies. The sympathetic looks from friends who'd warned her, the embarrassing conversations with family, the colleagues to whom she had introduced him as a fellow architect. The shame had been almost worse than the heartbreak.

She'd promised herself to be smarter, more cautious. Yet here she was again, emotionally invested in someone whose most basic claims she couldn't verify.

Julia's phone rang, startling her from her thoughts. Eliza's name flashed on the screen.

"Hey," she answered, trying to sound normal.

"Morning, Miss Raven. Just checking if we're still on for lunch?"

"I—" Julia hesitated. "Actually, could you come over instead? I need to talk to you about something."

Thirty minutes later, Eliza sat on Julia's sofa. "I understand I've been asked over to play a game of What's Wrong With Him."

"We don't know him that well."

"Good point. What *Could* Be Wrong With Him, then. You go first."

"What if he's married?"

"Too predictable. What else do you have?"

"What if he's a sex offender, just out of prison?"

Eliza raised both eyebrows meaningfully. "Now you're talking! Then be sure to check for ankle bracelet marks when you do meet."

"I'm serious, Eliza." Her friend then listened as Julia explained her fruitless search for The Black Tulip and her growing doubts about Dylan.

"Let me get this straight," Eliza said when Julia finished. "You've been talking to this guy for weeks, you have plans to meet in Boston, and you're just now doing basic research?"

"I know how it sounds," Julia admitted. "After Aaron, I should have been more careful."

"Don't disagree with you there," Eliza said. "So what

are you going to do?"

Julia gestured to her phone. "He keeps texting, asking if everything's okay. I don't know what to say."

"The truth would be a start," Eliza suggested. "His answer might tell you what you need to know. He might confess that he shops at Target, for instance."

"That's not funny. What if he just creates more elaborate lies? Aaron had an answer for everything."

"Then your radar will go up, and you cancel that part of the Boston meeting," Eliza said pragmatically. "But there could be a simple explanation. Not every business has an online presence."

"In 2025? An antique shop in a college town catering to affluent clients?" Julia shook her head.

"Well...I thought the whole point of Dylan was that he's stuck in the 1800s," Eliza said.

"So was Jack the Ripper," said Julia.

"That's more like it," said Eliza, "Though I'd prefer my serial killers to at least send flowers."

After Eliza left, Julia sat with her phone in hand, reading Dylan's latest message:

Dylan: *Julia, it's been nearly 24 hours since you responded. I'm genuinely concerned. If I've done something to upset you, please tell me. If you need space, I understand—just let me know you're alright.*

His sincerity made this harder. Either he was genuinely

concerned, or he was an exceptional manipulator. She had thought the same about Aaron, once.

Taking a deep breath, Julia began typing:

Julia: I'm sorry for going silent. I've been doing some thinking. When I tried to look up The Black Tulip, I couldn't find a single thing—no website, business listings, or reviews. This made me realize how little I can verify about your life. I had a rough experience with someone who wasn't honest about who he was, and now I'm having second thoughts.

Her finger hovered over the send button. Was she overreacting? Making accusations based on her past rather than her present? She pressed send before she could reconsider.

The response indicators appeared immediately, showing Dylan was typing. Then they disappeared. Then appeared again. Nearly five minutes passed before his message came through:

Dylan: I understand why you're concerned. The shop's lack of online presence was my uncle's approach. Clients found us through word of mouth.

Julia read the message, frowning. It felt evasive.

Julia: Your uncle's approach? Is he still involved in the business?

Another long pause.

Dylan: He passed away recently. I'm still figuring things out.

Julia: I'm sorry for your loss. How recently?

Dylan: Few months ago.

Julia waited for more details, but none came.

Julia: That must be difficult. Was it sudden?

Dylan: Unexpected.

Julia: Dylan, I can tell this is hard. But your answers feel . . . evasive. I'm just trying to understand why I can't find any trace of your shop anywhere.

Dylan: As I said, Uncle Tobias had an exclusive clientele.

Julia: But surely there would be some record? Business registration? Tax records? Something?

Dylan: There are records, Julia. Just not online ones.

Julia stared at her phone, her frustration growing. Every answer raised more questions.

Julia: I'm not trying to pry. I just need to feel comfortable about meeting someone I've only known through text messages.

Dylan: I wish I could explain everything better. It's complicated right now.

Julia: Complicated how?

No response came for several minutes. When it did, it was brief:

Dylan: I'm still trying to sort out some things about his death. It's been a labyrinth of complications.

Julia felt a pang of sympathy. She was also wary. His

pain seemed genuine, but so had Aaron's fabricated family emergencies.

Julia: I understand grief is private. But try to understand my position too. I'm about to meet someone whose business doesn't seem to exist, whose family situation is vague, at best . . .

Dylan: I don't blame you for being cautious.

Julia: Then help me understand. Give me something I can verify.

Another long pause.

Dylan: I can't right now. There are pending legal issues . . . I know how that sounds.

It sounded exactly like the kind of excuse someone would use to avoid providing proof, Julia thought. Yet something in his tone—the reluctance rather than defensiveness—gave her pause.

Julia: Legal issues related to your uncle's death?

Dylan: Among other things.

Julia: Dylan, this conversation is making me nervous.

Dylan: I know. I'm truly sorry. I want to tell you more, but can't right now. If you decide not to meet in Boston, I'll understand.

His response felt resigned. Either he was telling some version of the truth, or he was an exceptionally skilled liar.

Julia: I need to think about this.

Dylan: *Take all the time you need.*

As Julia set her phone down, she felt more conflicted than before. Dylan's evasiveness about his shop could mean he wasn't being straight with her. It also fit with someone dealing with a recent loss, and the messy aftermath. If his uncle really had just died, that could explain why he was being distant and why his business might be in some kind of legal tangle.

And yet, she couldn't shake the feeling that there were pieces of the story he wasn't telling her. Important pieces. Whether those omissions were protective or deceptive, she could not tell.

The night before her flight to Boston, Julia sat in bed, suitcase packed, presentation rehearsed. She hadn't confirmed or canceled their meeting. Eventually, she turned out the light and tried to sleep, knowing tomorrow would take her to Boston—and to a decision she wasn't yet prepared to make.

CHAPTER 7

The Quinn Alternative

The Boston Conference Center bustled with architects, preservationists, and sustainability experts from across the country. Julia adjusted her name badge and looked around, trying to focus on the conference program. In a few hours, she would be presenting her warehouse adaptive reuse project to a room full of peers.

"Ready for the big reveal?" Eliza appeared beside her, balancing two coffees. She handed one to Julia.

"Thanks," Julia said, gratefully accepting the cup. "I keep revising mental notes for the presentation."

"You know the project inside out. You're going to blow them away," Eliza assured her. "I'm more worried about the headhunters."

Eliza leaned closer to Julia amidst the conference chatter, her expression earnest. "Honestly, Julia, you're that rare hot commodity—the smart cookie with a sustainable heart. I've already seen a couple of headhunter types sniffing around."

Julia laughed, a light, confident sound. "Not a chance, Eliza. I'm perfectly happy where I am."

Eliza grinned. "That's what everyone says before they see the number on the signing bonus."

Julia smiled. This was vintage Eliza. Changing the game for your benefit. Sometimes, (but only sometimes), Julia wished she could be more like Eliza, breezing into a room like a geothermal vent just sprang open – all radiant energy and a hint of something volatile simmering beneath the surface.

Just then, Eliza squeezed Julia's arm. "Rock your presentation first, then we worry about Dylan."

Quinn approached, tablet in hand. "In case your anxious heart is curious, the projector in your room is actually working."

"The original mentalist," Julia said. "Thanks, Quinn."

"Just reading the signs, Jewels."

If Julia had a lifetime subscription to Murphy's law, Quinn was her exact opposite. He subscribed to Sunny's Law. If a person so much as walked in the direction of a beach, Quinn believed, the sun would be shining, beach towel in hand. Of course the projector was working.

"Think of everyone in this room as a nail," Quinn went on. "And you're the hammer."

"If I'm a hammer, you're the loose screw!" Julia joked. She had to admit that even amidst a crowd of well-dressed professionals, Quinn commanded attention. His sharply tailored charcoal suit accentuated his broad shoulders. A pristine white shirt peeked from beneath the jacket. And there was that distinctive crooked smile that grew slowly as it spread across his face, creating subtle lines around his eyes.

"We'll be in the front row sending supportive telepathic messages," he said, before walking away with Eliza. "I need to focus on the presentation," Julia said. "See you in a couple of hours."

After they had left, Julia checked the time on her phone. She had time to walk back to her hotel and freshen up. Just then, her phone chimed. It was a message from Dylan. She willed herself not to look at it. She should not do this to herself. She put her phone in her briefcase and made her way toward the entrance.

========

The time finally came.

As she was being introduced, Julia stood at the bottom of the stairs. Quinn, Eliza and Martin were seated in the front row. Eliza did a little friendly wave, Quinn winked at her, and Martin gave her two thumbs up. Julia smiled toward them, grateful for their presence in her life. These were her people. They were part of her often reflections on seeking and finding. They were together every day, working toward something they found meaningful. These were the ones who asked, "How are you, really?" Sometimes Julia wondered what would happen to her life if they were not in it.

Right before her presentation, she thought about Dylan's message. But she was here now. She had to focus.

"...which allowed us to preserve 78% of the original structural elements while achieving modern energy efficiency standards." Julia advanced to her final slide, a rendering of the completed warehouse project. "The result will be a building that honors its industrial heritage while serving contemporary needs—proving that preservation and progress can coexist. I'll take your questions now."

Applause filled the room. During the Q&A session, she fielded questions with confidence, drawing on her intimate knowledge of the building's history and the restoration challenges.

Afterwards, a few attendees came up to her to compliment her presentation. A small queue formed. One man stood out – sharp suit and graying temples hinting at experience. He had the air of someone not used to standing in line, unless he had a good reason to do so. Across the room, Eliza caught Julia's eye and mouthed a dramatic, silent, "Poacher!" Julia fought to keep a professional smile on her face as the man extended his hand.

Quinn approached last, waiting until the crowd had thinned and gave her a fist bump. "You had everyone under your spell."

"Thanks! Looks like it went well."

"Well? You crushed it," he insisted. "The way you connected historical significance with contemporary function—that's the kind of thinking we need now, seriously."

His flattery was grounding. Here was someone who understood her work, appreciated her perspective, and shared her professional values.

"By the by, are you free for dinner tonight?" Quinn asked. "A few of us were planning to try that new place in the hotel—Harvest, I think it's called."

Julia hesitated. If she had dinner with Quinn and colleagues, she'd have a perfect excuse not to meet Dylan. After much debate, she had decided that she was not ready.

"That sounds nice," she said. "What time?"

"Seven-thirty?"

"Count me in," she said, with a mixture of relief and guilt.

As Quinn walked away, Julia checked her phone. There had been no new messages from Dylan after wishing her luck in her presentation. Julia had told him she'd touch base with him afterwards, but she had not texted him yet. The afternoon passed in a blur of sessions, professional networking, and deliberate distractions that pushed thoughts of Dylan to the edges of her consciousness. By the time she returned to her room to change for dinner, she felt almost normal—focused on the conference and on the professional opportunities surrounding her.

Until she checked her phone and saw the message:

Dylan: *I hope your presentation went well! I arrived in Boston early. Still hoping we might meet, but understand if you've changed your mind. Staying at the Hawthorne Inn.*

Julia sat on the edge of the bed, the carefully constructed compart-mentalization of her day was falling apart.

She began typing a response:

I'm sorry, Dylan. Recent events have made me question whether this is a good idea.

She deleted it and tried again:

My presentation went well, thank you! I've made dinner plans with colleagues tonight. I don't think meeting will work out.

Still not right. Too cold, too dismissive of everything they'd shared. She started over:

Dylan, I'm still processing our last conversation. While I appreciate your explanation, I need more time to think about meeting in person. Could we postpone?

Her finger hovered over the send button when a knock at her door startled her. She set the phone down without sending the message. Eliza was at the door, already dressed for dinner.

"Are you not getting my messages?" Eliza asked. "We're meeting in the lobby in fifteen minutes." She then noticed Julia's expression. "What's wrong?"

"Dylan's already in Boston."

"Whaaa . . . ?" Eliza said, stepping into the room. "And you're freaking out."

"I'm not freaking out," Julia said. "I'm just . . . reassessing."

"While Quinn waits downstairs," Eliza said, squinting dramatically.

"It's a group dinner," Julia said. "Not a date!"

"Right ... right," Eliza drawled. "And Quinn just happened to mention three times how much he's looking forward to continuing your earlier conversation."

Julia sighed, sitting at the small desk. "I just wish Quinn weren't so..."

"Verifiable?" Eliza said, fixing Julia with one of her sideway glances.

"I mean predictable. There's no mystery to him, nothing new to know... He's just a normal, straightforward co-worker who happens to be interested."

"And he's so so safe," Eliza added.

"What do you mean?"

"Quinn's the safe bet. You work together, you understand each other's worlds, so there's a kind of ... pseudo-intimacy between you two. Though that's not the same as love. You know that feeling you get when you're falling at high speed inside an elevator that's come unhinged? It's the best feeling ever. And I want that for you, Jewels."

"I don't like the word 'unhinged.' And you know that's a myth. Elevators don't come unhinged. The emergency brakes engage automatically if the car starts to fall."

"You took words out of my mouth! You're applying the emergency brake before anything happens with Quinn."

Julia was silent, absorbing Eliza's perspective.

"Look," Eliza continued, more gently, "Quinn is great. If you're genuinely interested in him, fantastic. But if you're choosing him because he's the safer option after Aaron hurt you, that's not fair to either of you. Or to Dylan, for that matter."

"I don't know what I want," Julia admitted.

"That's the first honest thing you've said all day," Eliza said. "Get dressed for dinner. You don't have to make any decisions tonight."

========

Pendant lights cast a warm glow throughout the elegant Harvest restaurant. Julia was seated between Quinn and Martin, with Eliza across the table beside two other colleagues from the firm.

Quinn was the perfect dinner companion—attentive without hovering, knowledgeable about many things, funny without trying too hard. When the server went on a pretentious monologue about the fish of the day, Quinn whispered to Julia, "Translation: it's fish on a plate with stuff on it."

By the time dessert arrived, Julia was really enjoying his company. The simplicity of their connection was appealing—no need to explain industry terms or translate professional challenges. He understood her world because he lived in it too.

As they walked out of the restaurant, Quinn said, "Some of us are heading to the hotel bar for a nightcap. Care to join?"

"I should probably turn in early," she said. "It's been a long day."

"You were amazing today! Get some rest."

"Thank you for everything—checking the projector, the jokes," she said.

"That's what friends are for."

As soon as she got to her room, Julia sat on the bed and checked her phone. No new messages from Dylan.

She decided to answer him:

Julia: *Sorry for not responding sooner. My presentation went well. Thanks for letting me know you're in Boston early. I'll text you some breakfast options in a bit.*

She headed to the bathroom for a much-needed shower. Under the running water, Julia couldn't find a name for what was shaking her as if she would break. It was too late, she thought. She could never get her old self back, could not reclaim herself from the emptiness of betrayal. Was she condemned to live with this open wound forever? A knot of tears started traveling up her throat. Technically, her life had continued after Aaron. But could she ever trust anyone again?

CHAPTER 8

Duck Tours and Revelations

Wisteria Café occupied the ground floor of a restored brownstone on Commonwealth Avenue, its bay windows streaming late morning sunlight onto marble-topped tables. Julia had chosen it deliberately—public enough to feel safe, charming enough to be memorable if things went well. She arrived fifteen minutes early, selecting a corner table with a view of both the entrance and the street, where blooming magnolias softened the elegant architecture of Back Bay.

She smoothed her emerald silk blouse, second-guessing her outfit choice for perhaps the tenth time that morning. The blouse, dark jeans, and ankle boots had seemed the right balance of casual and polished in her hotel room, but now she wondered if she should have worn something more distinctive.

The server, a young woman with intricate braids and wire-rimmed glasses, approached with a friendly smile. "Welcome to Wisteria. Can I get you started with something?"

"Sparkling water for now," Julia replied. "I'm waiting for someone."

"I'll bring that right out."

Julia checked her watch. Five minutes to their agreed time—11 a.m.

The bell above the door chimed, and Julia looked up. Dylan walked in. He was taller than she expected, his dark hair freshly tousled from the spring breeze. He wore a blue shirt that hugged broad shoulders, jeans, and boots that had been broken in through actual wear, rather than artificial distressing.

For a moment he stood framed in the doorway, scanning the café until his eyes found hers. The growing smile that transformed his serious expression made Julia feel a little less self-conscious. Still, her throat felt dry. Despite weeks of intimate conversation, Julia was suddenly shy.

Dylan moved toward her table with purpose, navigating between chairs with the fluidity of someone comfortable in his physical space.

"Julia," he said, in a rich, deep voice. Those blue eyes she'd seen in photos were sharper in real life, crinkled slightly at the corners when he smiled.

"Dylan," she said, standing to greet him, not sure of the appropriate gesture. A handshake seemed too formal, a hug might be too much. Her dark hair was pulled back in a messy bun, a few tendrils escaping to frame her face, highlighting the smattering of freckles across her nose.

He took her in, then touched her forearm gently, a gesture that bridged the gap between formality and intimacy. "I'm glad you came. It's so great to finally meet you in person."

"You too," Julia said, surprised by how genuinely she meant it despite her reservations.

They sat, both feeling awkward as they managed the adjustment to the reality of physical presence after weeks of digital connection.

"This is strange, isn't it?" she admitted, tucking a strand of hair behind her ear. "After all our chats, I'm suddenly tongue-tied."

"Same here," Dylan said. "I had this whole mental list of things I wanted to tell you, and now I can't remember any of them."

"Maybe we should start with something non-threatening," Julia smiled. "Like . . . how was your train ride?"

Dylan laughed—a rich sound that sent an unexpected flutter through her. "The train was fine, though I spent the entire ride wondering if you'd actually show up."

"I almost didn't," Julia admitted. "I've been second-guessing this decision since I sent that message."

"And now that you're here?" Dylan asked, his eyes searching her face.

Just then, the server returned with her sparkling water and turned to Dylan. "Can I get you something to drink?"

"Do you have French press coffee?" he asked.

"Medium or dark roast?"

"Dark, please," Dylan said. "And I'm ready to order if you are?" he added, looking at Julia.

"I'll need another minute," she said.

Once the server walked away, Dylan leaned forward. "I have a confession to make."

Julia's guard went up. Here it comes, she thought. "Oh?"

"I was so nervous about meeting you that I forgot to eat breakfast," he said with a self-deprecating smile. "Now I'm both starving and trying to play it cool."

His admission disarmed her. "That makes two of us," Julia said. "I had coffee in my hotel room but couldn't manage anything else."

"Presentation nerves on top of everything else?"

"Actually, the presentation went well yesterday," Julia said. "Really well, in fact. There was more interest in the warehouse project than I had expected."

"I'm not surprised," Dylan said. His eyes were attentive,

with the right amount of intensity. "Congratulations."

They ordered—avocado toast for Julia, a breakfast croissant for Dylan.

The late-morning light streamed through the large windows, painting the exposed brick walls in a warm glow.

"Beautiful place," Dylan said, looking around at the pressed tin ceiling, the antique botanical prints on walls painted a soft sage and the marble countertops.

"I thought you might appreciate it," she said. "The owners preserved most of the original architectural elements when they renovated."

She was grateful for architecture. Objects were so easy to talk about. Julia had many questions for Dylan but decided to wait. They had a whole day ahead of them. Time enough to determine if the man sitting across from her was what he seemed.

When their food arrived, Julia took a bite and said it was the perfect avocado.

Across from her, Dylan began to meticulously dissect his croissant.

"You look like you're performing surgery on that croissant," Julia said, smiling.

Dylan looked up. "Achieving the perfect bite is an art form."

"A messy art form, in this case," Julia teased, nodding towards the small pile of crumbs accumulating on his plate.

At that moment, a harried-looking server, balancing a precarious tower of dirty plates, bumped into their table. Dylan's ice water glass teetered and then, with agonizing slowness, tipped over, sending a small wave of water across the table. It landed squarely on Julia's lap.

"Oh, no! I am so, so incredibly sorry!" the server gasped, his eyes wide with horror.

Julia yelped. "Whoa! That's ... " She blinked down to look at the dark, spreading wetness on her jeans. It was pooling uncomfortably. It was also cold.

Dylan shot up right away and grabbed a handful of napkins from their table. "Are you okay?"

Dylan, who could identify a Bordeaux by its terroir and had once coaxed a stubborn red wine stain out of a cream-colored rug using a combination of salt and club soda, approached the spill cautiously. Secretly, he was waging a small war—to rub, or not to rub. When it came to red wine, the key was not to rub, (which would only spread the stain), but to apply firm, direct pressure. But water on a live body was different. How to help without encroaching on Julia's jeans?

"Here," he said, handing her the extra napkins. "Tactical blotting is key."

His touch was ... unexpectedly nice, Julia thought, for a quick second.

"Tactical blotting?" she smiled, taking the napkins.

He was now standing beside her, careful to maintain a

safe distance from her lap. A few nearby patrons were now observing the situation.

For her part, Julia was trying to discreetly absorb the water with the napkins, without calling attention to her inner thigh. "Wet jeans are a fashion statement," she said, looking up at Dylan.

"Wetly distressed," he smiled.

The server, having mopped up the worst of the spill, offered profuse apologies and a complimentary pastry. Julia and Dylan both waved him off, their attention back on each other.

"So," Julia said, picking up her fork again, "About tactical blotting."

"It's all about knowing when *not* to rub," he said, smiling.

"When not to rub," she smiled back.

"You have to be gentle," Dylan said, locking eyes with her.

"Exactly."

"And patient."

"Yes," said Julia. "Patience is key."

"It's all about textile preservation."

"I know what you mean," she said.

Despite the sobering splash and the many unanswered questions, Julia felt a subtle shift in her. The day was still unfolding and something like hope was growing inside her.

Outside, Commonwealth Avenue stretched before them, lined with trees just beginning to leaf out. Julia was grateful for the late morning sun. The dark patch on her jeans looked less stark as it started to dry. Dylan, a head taller than her, moved with an easy stride along the bustling sidewalks.

"Where are we off to now?" Julia asked, stopping at the corner.

"Do you trust me?" Dylan asked, stopping next to her.

"What did you have in mind?"

"Close your eyes and give me your hand," he said.

He reached into his shirt's pocket, placed two tickets on her hand and said, "You can open them now."

Julia looked at two bright yellow tickets and raised an eyebrow. Then her lips curled into an amused smile.

Dylan made a sweeping gesture toward the city. "I thought we should go to a place where we could see Boston from a *whole* new perspective . . . both on land and, quite literally, on water. We're going on a Duck Tour."

"A duck tour?" Julia shook her head and looked up at him. His blue eyes glinty under the sun.

"A true Boston rite of passage," Dylan said.

They walked for a leisurely fifteen minutes, the city unfolding around them like a living history book. The air hummed with the sounds of traffic, the distant clang of a trolley bell, and snippets of conversations in a multitude of accents. The aroma of freshly baked bread wafted from an open bakery door.

As they rounded a corner near the New England Aquarium, the yellow and green of the Duck Boat came into view. It was an odd contraption, its tall, sturdy wheels giving it the height of a bus, but its rounded hull and open top hinted at its aquatic capabilities. Playful cartoon ducks were painted along the sides, adding a whimsical touch to the military-esque vehicle.

"That," Dylan said, gesturing toward it with a flourish, "is our chariot. Or should I say, our *quacking* chariot." He grinned, eager to see her reaction.

Julia was very curious about this; her eyes noticed the details of things.

A cheerful crowd was milling around the boarding area. But since Dylan had already bought their tickets, they were directed by a friendly attendant toward the boarding area.

"See those? Dylan said, pointing to the large tires. Great on the road. But the real fun starts when we drive straight into the Charles."

Julia laughed, the novelty of the situation starting to win her over. "Drive *into* the river? You're not pulling my leg, are you?"

"Wouldn't dream of it," Dylan said.

As they climbed aboard the quirky vehicle, they settled into open-air seats next to each other, occasionally brushing hands. Neither resisted. When they splashed into the Charles River, the spray of water brought them closer still, both laughing at the unexpected jolt.

"This is so beautiful," Julia said, looking at the sailboats. "So different from Savannah."

"What was it like, growing up there?"

Julia squinted. "The pace is … slower, I think. Definitely steeped in history, but in a different way. Spanish moss hanging from ancient oaks, the scent of gardenias in the air. Summers are long and humid, fireflies in the evenings. Growing up, we spent a lot of time near the water. But the water is very different—marshy, tidal creeks instead of a wide river like this one." She told Dylan about the horse-drawn carriages, the antebellum architecture, and the taste of sweet tea on a porch swing.

"Sounds like a place that would never let you go," Dylan said softly. "Would you ever leave, do you think?"

"There's a weight to Savannah, for sure. But there's also a certain languor, a slower pace that sometimes feels …"

Her gaze drifted towards the Charles River, the sunlight glinting on the water. "That's a good question … I've thought about it from time to time." She turned back to him. "It's home, you know. The sound of cicadas in the summer, those things are ingrained. But there are other things, too; a chance to build something new, maybe …" Her voice trailed off, her eyes meeting his.

Dylan's breath hitched slightly. He was from Rhode Island, a place close enough to Boston to feel like a possibility, a bridge. The way Julia talked about Savannah, though, made the place feel impossibly far away. "What kind of new?" he asked, his voice low over the rumble of the boat engine.

Julia was about to say something, but didn't get a chance. The duck boat rumbled back, and the tour guide's voice announced the return to land.

Dylan hopped out, landing with surprising agility for his height. Then, turning back to Julia, a playful glint in his eyes, he reached out, his hands finding her waist. In a swift, unexpected move, he lifted her as if she were lighter than a leaf. Her surprised gasp was lost in the breeze. For a moment, suspended in the air, her eyes locked with his and she felt her world had shifted a little.

As they disembarked, Dylan's hand found hers naturally, their fingers intertwining as if they'd done this hundreds of times before. Julia felt a small thrill at the contact—the warmth of his palm against hers, the gentle pressure of his thumb occasionally brushing her wrist.

They wandered down Charles Street, stopping occasionally to browse in shops—an antiquarian bookstore where Julia found a rare volume on colonial architecture that made her eyes light up, then a small art gallery featuring local artists' interpretations of Boston landmarks. Their eyes met every now and again, as if verifying the other was still there.

"My uncle would have loved this place," Dylan said, as

they left the bookstore.

"Dylan," Julia said gently as they continued walking, "I know this is difficult. But I think you owe me an explanation."

His stride faltered slightly. "About what?"

"About your uncle. About why you couldn't give me straight answers when I asked about The Black Tulip." She stopped walking, turning to face him.

Dylan's jaw tightened. For a moment, Julia thought he might deflect again. Instead, he looked around, spotting a small park overlooking the Charles River. "It would probably be better if we sat down for this."

They found a bench facing the water. Dylan leaned forward, elbows on his knees, staring straight ahead.

"You're right," he started. "I do owe you an explanation." His voice was low, strained. "Uncle Tobias didn't just die, Julia. The circumstances were . . ." He swallowed hard. "They were suspicious."

Julia arched her back. "Suspicious how?"

"He was in Istanbul, chasing a treasure he'd been obsessed with finding for the past six years—a first edition of 'The Black Tulip' by Alexandre Dumas—that's what our shop is named after—so this collector claimed to have not just any first edition, but one that had belonged to Dumas himself."

"And?"

"My uncle called me the night before he was supposed to meet this collector. He was so excited, Julia. Said it was finally happening, that he could feel it." Dylan's voice cracked slightly. "But tomorrow never came. The next day, they found him dead in his hotel room."

"Oh my God, Dylan," Julia leaned forward and gave his forearm a gentle squeeze.

"But here's the thing—the collector vanished. No record of any meeting. No trace of the correspondence that had brought my uncle there. The hotel staff gave conflicting stories about whether he'd had visitors."

Dylan straightened and faced Julia, his blue eyes glistening. "I flew to Istanbul right away. But the authorities had already closed the case. American businessman, advanced age, natural causes."

"And that's not what you think happened?" Julia said.

"I don't know what to think anymore. This has been consuming in a way that is hard to explain. I haven't slept through the night for a while." Dylan's voice was low and raw. "Maybe it was just a heart attack. Maybe the collector was real but got spooked. Or maybe . . ." He trailed off, shaking his head.

Julia tried searching for the right words. But none came.

"The worst part is not knowing," Dylan said. "This isn't just about The Black Tulip. Uncle Tobias was everything to me—mentor, business partner, father figure. He raised me after my father died. And I'll never know if his obsession with that damn book got the best of him, or if I'm just imagining conspiracies where there are none. You can see why this is not something I want to talk about."

Julia felt tears prick her eyes. "Yes."

"Especially to you."

"To me?"

"I joined the wine forum as a distraction. For a while, my uncle's death was all I could think about. It was pretty rough. Then you came along. From your very first post, I just knew. I knew you were someone who could matter too much. You don't have to read through a lot of threads to know what's what. And I loved that about you. I loved that you believe that every scrap of metal, every crumbled brick and dusty pipe could be rearranged into something beautiful. And for a little while, I allowed myself to believe that happiness was possible."

Julia's heart ached for him. She looked at him – the grief that had settled on his features the only barrier to his strikingly handsome face.

"Dylan," she said softly, "I'm so sorry. For your loss, for pushing you when you weren't ready."

"Don't be," he said, softly. "Julia, you're so much more than I had ever hoped for." His touch was gentle when he lifted her chin. Though they had been looking at each other all day, Julia felt this was the first time she felt the full impact of his eyes on her.

"Thank you for trusting me with this," Julia said.

"I'm glad I did," Dylan replied. He brought her hand to his lips and started kissing each fingertip slowly, gently, one by one, one at a time, his eyes closed. Julia, too, closed her eyes and thought that if there was a reason to be alive, it was on the chance you'd get to experience a moment like this; a moment where you could feel every feeling: sadness, joy, heartache, hope, relief, and the feeling that the person sitting next to you found you so hard to believe, so much greater than they had ever imagined. She was happy. She was hopeful. Julia thought she might weep.

They left the park, their steps weaving a silent rhythm through the softening light of dusk, hands interlaced as they walked towards Julia's hotel. The world around them was dissolving, slowly, into hues of gold, and with each shared breath, Julia felt their connection growing. When his fingers tightened around hers, a comforting warmth traveled through her. Life, she thought, was undeniably complex, much of it uncertain. Yet, at this moment, she was grateful to have risked her heart on someone like Dylan Gilbert. He was generous and kind, and more real than she had allowed herself to imagine.

They must have decided at the same time: that they didn't want this day to end. So they slowed down the pace, holding hands, neither talking for a long while.

Eventually, they reached her hotel. Dylan turned to face Julia, his expression soft in the faint street light.

"Thank you for today," he said, caressing her cheek.

"For taking a chance on meeting me."

"Thank you for being exactly who I hoped you were," Julia replied, surprising herself with her candor. Dylan's lips approached hers slowly, a question mark in his eyes. But as Julia responded, the kiss deepened, his hand cradling her face with exquisite tenderness. Time seemed to hold still as the connection between them transformed yet again; this time, into something deeply intimate. Julia felt slightly breathless, her heart racing with a mixture of desire and wonder, a soft flush rising to her cheeks. Dylan's eyes were darker now, his gaze intense.

"Dinner tomorrow?" he asked.

"I wish," Julia replied. "I have an early flight."

He ran the back of his finger tenderly across her cheek once again, a gesture so affectionate it made Julia's heart ache. He leaned in, his lips brushing her ear as he spoke.

"This isn't the end, Julia," he whispered, his breath sending a shiver through her.

She nodded, a smile breaking through the disappointment of their farewell. He drew her close for another kiss, a tender, lingering embrace that made Julia wish they could stay here forever. As she watched him walk away into the lamplit night, a feeling close to hope came to her, something she hadn't experienced in the longest time. Whatever happened next—however they navigated the complexity of distance and separate lives—the connection they had formed was beautifully real.

Tomorrow would bring new possibilities, new discoveries. But tonight, with the warmth of Dylan's kiss lingering on her lips, Julia allowed herself to dream again. On the way to her room, she played a conversation game inside her head. She wouldn't necessarily have guessed the words that would come tumbling out of his mouth. It should not be too hard to guess.

"Is that *really* how you two met?"

"More or less," he'd say, a private smile on his lips.

"More, or less?" Julia's voice echoed.

"Well," he'd say, a twinkle in his eye, "It certainly wasn't over a candlelit dinner. Or going after the same lemon at the market."

"I don't know anymore," her imagined self would say.

"Neither do I," he'd agree, his gaze meeting hers across the table. "All I remember is . . . it was definitely a vintage year."

"A very good vintage," she'd say. And someone at the table would finally piece it together, "So, it was a wine thing then?"

"More or less."

CHAPTER 9

The Breaking Point

Three weeks after leaving Boston, Julia found herself unexpectedly busy. Her warehouse renovation project had caught the attention of many people, including Westover & Crane, one of Boston's premier architectural preservation firms. Suddenly, her inbox was filled with questions, consulting offers and more attention than she wanted. What she wanted was to work during normal business hours, go out with friends, enjoy a glass of wine and go to bed at a decent time. On the rare occasion that she left work before dark, she was exhausted. Among the casualties of this overload was her relationship with Dylan, which had started to feel like a dream she had while on vacation.

Recently, their conversations had become increasingly strained, increasingly infrequent, increasingly detached.

One night, while Julia was heating up leftovers, Dylan called. She was still in her work clothes. She didn't feel like talking. It was a mistake to pick up the phone.

"Hey!" Dylan said.

"Hey."

"Is this a good time?"

"As good as any."

"Are you okay?"

"Just tired."

He let out a deep sigh. "You sound more than just tired, Julia. What's the matter?"

"Why can't you leave anything alone?" she asked. Julia knew when a conversation was about to turn. But she couldn't stop herself.

"Because I can tell something's wrong. Why are you so guarded?"

"Look who's talking about being guarded."

"This isn't about me, Julia."

She set the phone on the kitchen counter and kept stirring the rice.

"It is about you!" she snapped. "You're the one who's afraid to open up, who wants to live surrounded by objects, afraid of real people, and putting me in a situation I never wanted to be in."

"Well, I'm sorry if you think I have something terminal for being private. Life isn't one of your projects, Julia. Sometimes you can't line up the beams and end up with a brand-new building. Sometimes, you have to walk out of the rubble and try to make sense of what you lost in the fire."

"Do that, then," she said, her voice rattled.

She just needed to get to the end of the week and her life would get back to normal.

"You know this isn't about me, Julia," Dylan said. "You're the one avoiding my calls."

"You're right! I don't think I have the energy for this anymore. Good night, Dylan."

"Goodbye, Julia."

Her hands were shaking. Her apartment was humid and hot. She needed time to think, to refocus, to figure out where to take her life next. She hadn't counted on Dylan taking her at her word.

========

This wasn't working, Dylan thought. He couldn't go on like this; not sleeping, perpetually holding his breath, indefinitely postponing the looming task of sorting through the rooms of his uncle's house.

Since his uncle's death, Dylan hadn't been able to bring himself to enter the place that was like a second home to him. The abrupt ending with Julia and the lawyer's letters about the estate, had finally forced his hand.

He wore his oldest jeans and a faded t-shirt. He was sweaty and grimy from hours of sorting through his uncle's personal effects in the Beacon Hill townhouse; a place now stripped bare of the presence of the man who had stood watch over his life.

On the mahogany roll-top desk, everything lay in precise order: a worn leather-bound journal, a pair of reading spectacles, and a small pocket watch that caught the afternoon light streaming through the study's windows. Slowly, methodically, Dylan had started sorting everything out, creating piles on the Persian rug beneath his feet: keep, donate, discard. For the most part, his uncle received business correspondence at The Black Tulip. Here, at his home, were his personal belongings. In the bottom right cubby, alongside a stick of red sealing wax and a brass seal, Dylan noticed an envelope.

His own name written in his uncle's precise handwriting, with a notation in the corner: To be opened after my death.

Dylan took a deep breath and turned the envelope over. He broke the seal carefully and unfolded two sheets of cream-colored stationary.

My dear Dylan,

If you are reading this, then I finally ran out of borrowed time. A few months ago, Dr. Morrison had warned me about my weak heart. I chose not to burden you with that knowledge. Perhaps this makes me a coward. You see, I have spent my entire life being cautious, afraid of getting close to anything too personal.

Dylan sat on one of the leather chairs beside the desk.

He felt suddenly unsteady.

You knew all about my quest for that first edition, about my plans to go to Istanbul – a man chasing a shadow across an ocean for a book that may not have existed.

On the day you lost your father, I lost my brother to a heart condition that became my life's condition. I also lost my nerve. I was too afraid to die like him.

So I spent sixty-two years searching for the perfect thing—the perfect antique, the perfect bottle of wine, the perfect moment to take a real risk. Distractions are a marvelous way to avoid life. It is shockingly easy to distract yourself, my boy. I told myself I was building something important, preserving history, creating a legacy. But the truth pokes holes in this mythology of mine. I spent my life hiding behind beautiful objects. Objects don't talk back. Objects don't protest. They could never disappoint me the way people might.

I was madly, irrevocably, helplessly in love with Cecila Barnes. But did I ever tell her? Did I ever invite her to dinner? The risk of her laughing in my face was more than I could bear. A couple of times we went into my cellar and I gave her a bottle. One time, she looked me in the eye and joked: "Tobias, perhaps I should just move in!" You can say that I died without finding the right words for Cecilia.

The Black Tulip became my obsession, not because of its rarity, but because it represented everything I thought I needed to finally start living – one last perfect acquisition to justify a lifetime of waiting for the perfect moment.

But there is no perfect moment. There is no perfect love, no perfect opportunity – life is the opportunity!

The shop . . . the building . . . my house . . . and a wine cellar that could drown a small village —these are all yours now. Use what I have left you to build something real. And if you spot a Cecilia anywhere, push the limits of hope and courage. Don't chase a phantom flower when a real one is blooming in front of your eyes.

The doctors will tell you that I died of a heart condition. And this would be true. My heart gave out from so much regret. And from realizing, too late, that the most valuable things are usually the most fragile.

Please give my love to Cecilia when you see her next. On second thought, what could she do with that information now?

All my love,

Uncle Tobias

Dylan read the letter twice before setting it down on the desk and walked up to the window. The sun was getting ready to call it a day. What wouldn't he give to hear his uncle's voice again in the stillness of his study.

A coward. Uncle Tobias called himself a coward. He stood still, trying to reconcile this letter with the man he had known—the tall antiquarian with the mop of silver hair who held people rapt with stories of Revolutionary War currency and Victorian mourning jewelry. His uncle was someone Dylan had admired for his knowledge of history, of wine, for his certainty about the world. That he had been as lost as Dylan felt right now, was hard to believe.

The late afternoon light shifted, casting longer shadows across the Persian rug. Dylan's chest felt tight. He could see himself in parts of that letter—the careful calculations, the endless postponements. He pressed his palms against his eyes and let out the longest breath. This was a lot to absorb—four months of questions answered, at last. But replaced by harder truths about courage, about the cost of playing it safe.

He stayed at the house until it grew dark. It was a wretched feeling, sitting alone with the resident ghosts. Cecilia Barnes. He couldn't believe it. He knew what he had to do

CHAPTER 10

The Perfect Pairing

Westover & Crane didn't let up. Julia had agreed to a phone interview, but only to confirm to herself that she was not interested in the job. She received a phone call from one of the partners, then another, and another. Still, Julia wasn't convinced. By month's end, a formal offer arrived. The salary made her eyes widen, but it was the challenging project list that made her heart race with excitement.

It was a far bigger decision than she'd anticipated—even for something she'd only dreamed about. Dreams rarely factor in the inconvenient details that must be overcome to make them a reality. Boston meant career advancement and more prestigious projects. Savannah meant home, her established network, and her cherished colleagues and friends. Professionally, it meant abandoning the historic warehouse project she'd poured her soul into for almost a year.

"I can't do it," she said to Eliza. "It's not just about the job," she confessed. "It's about you guys, too."

Eliza, perched on the armrest of Julia's sofa, unexpectedly softened. "Of course it is," she replied. "Missing your friends is allowed. It's practically a constitutional right when you're contemplating a move to, well, *Boston*." She shuddered theatrically.

Julia managed a weak smile. "But that doesn't make it any easier."

"No, it doesn't," Eliza agreed. "But are we talking 'miss you so much I'll send cornbread care packages,'?" She paused, then added, "Because that requires actual boxes. The other kind of missing just requires a good therapist and a decent broadband connection."

Julia laughed. It was a teary laugh, though. "What if I regret it? What if Boston just isn't . . . Savannah?"

Eliza squeezed her hand. "It won't be. It'll be colder, for a start. And they probably don't deep-fry enough things. But it'll also be *new*. And besides, you're too brilliant to stay comfortable forever. Be brave! We'll still be here, probably complaining about the humidity."

After her friend left, Julia walked toward the open window, the evening air a balm on her skin. Savannah was home. There was so much she would miss: the lull of Mrs. Mercer's voice, almost as comforting as her peach cobbler; the Spanish moss swaying gently in the breeze, and the chorus of crickets that had sung her to sleep. It was not easy, leaving a place where every breath felt like a memory.

Leaving it all for a job—would it truly be worth it? Julia needed time to think. The next day, an ordinary Wednesday, she asked for the afternoon off.

The afternoon heat hung over Savannah like a damp blanket. Mrs. Mercer's melodious drawl drifted across the veranda as Julia climbed the steps, her lightweight cotton blouse clinging to her back.

"You simply must come in for some lemonade," Mrs. Mercer was saying. She wore a flowing sundress in soft yellow, her silver hair pinned up. "She's a very busy girl, you know—she won't be home until late."

Julia paused on the bottom step. A pang of dread washed over her. Dr. Da Silva again, she thought. But something about the voice responding to Mrs. Mercer made her stop.

"You're so right. I should have called ahead." It was a rich, measured voice, very unlike Dr. Da Silva's cheerful chatter.

Julia's breath caught. She knew that voice. The man standing with his back to the stairs wore khaki chinos and a light blue linen shirt, the sleeves rolled up. His dark hair and broad shoulders were hard to miss.

"What lovely manners!" Mrs. Mercer continued. "When she does get home, I'll be sure to tell her what a distinguished gentleman came calling. Though I do wish you could stay—"

Dylan turned as she spoke, and their eyes met across

the veranda.

"Dylan!?" Slowly, Julia set the briefcase on the wooden steps.

"Juliaah," he smiled. His face transformed, relief and joy colliding in that devastating smile she'd been missing for weeks.

Mrs. Mercer's hands flew to her chest. "Well, I do declare! Julia, darling, you didn't tell me you had such a distinguished gentleman coming to visit!"

"I . . . didn't," Julia stammered, unable to look away from Dylan. "What are you doing here?"

"Something I should have done weeks ago," Dylan said, moving toward her.

"How wonderfully romantic," Mrs. Mercer said. "Like something from a Jane Austen novel!"

Julia bent to grab her briefcase, her mind racing. "You flew all the way to Savannah just to see me?"

"I flew to Savannah because I realized I was being an idiot." Dylan's honesty was disarming.

"Well," Mrs. Mercer interjected, "whatever brought you here, I approve wholeheartedly. Julia, invite this charming man upstairs this instant."

"Mrs. Mercer—" Julia began.

"No arguments, sweet pea. A man doesn't travel a thousand miles to stand on a porch making small talk." She fixed Dylan with a stern but affectionate look. "I do hope your intentions are honorable."

Dylan's ears reddened slightly. "The most honorable, ma'am."

Mrs. Mercer beamed. "Now you two go on upstairs before this heat melts us all into puddles."

Julia looked at Dylan, who was trying to hide his amusement. "You've been thoroughly Southern-mothered."

"Completely charmed by Southern hospitality," he said. "Mrs. Mercer has already offered me lemonade and asked detailed questions about my family tree."

"She works fast," Julia said, finally allowing herself to smile. "Would you like to come up? It's cooler inside."

"I thought you'd never ask!"

As they climbed the staircase to her apartment, Julia felt acutely aware of Dylan behind her—the warmth from his body, the sound of his breathing. At her door, she fumbled with the key.

"I'm so glad you're here," he said.

She turned to face him on the small landing, their bodies inches apart. "I'm really glad you came."

The apartment was cool, thanks to the ceiling fans. Dylan took in the exposed brick walls, the architectural drawings pinned to a large cork board, the material samples scattered across her dining table. He looked mesmerized by the reality of it.

"Can I get you something to drink? Water? Iced tea?" Julia set down her briefcase, suddenly nervous.

"Water would be great."

She busied herself in the kitchen, grateful for something to do with her hands.

"Dylan," she said, handing him the glass. "About our last phone call—"

"I owe you an apology," he said, setting the water down. "I was holding back, and I know you felt it."

"I was rude. I was busy and overwhelmed," she admitted, settling onto the couch.

He sat beside her, close enough that she could smell his cologne—something clean and understated. "I had been struggling with some personal things. And instead of trusting you, I pulled away."

"We both did." Julia said, tucked one leg beneath her. "I got scared."

"Of what?"

"Of getting hurt again."

Dylan reached for her hand, tracing circles on her palm with one of his fingers. "I would never hurt you intentionally, Julia. But I understand why you'd be cautious."

The contact with his hand sent shivers up her arm. "I've missed you," she whispered.

"You've no idea how I've missed you." His voice was

full of emotion. "These past few weeks have been hell."

Julia looked at his face—the intensity in his blue eyes, the slight stubble from travel, the way he looked at her like she was the rarest find. She got closer to him. His free hand cupped her face, thumb brushing across her cheek as he leaned in. The kiss was gentle at first. But when Julia's lips parted, inviting him deeper, something shifted between them.

Dylan's hand slid into her hair, auburn strands tangling as he gently pulled her closer. Julia's hands found the soft cotton of his shirt, gripping it lightly as their kiss deepened, months of longing pouring into this breathtaking moment. The world outside faded, leaving only the soft sighs that escaped them.

"God, Julia," Dylan murmured against her lips.

"Don't stop," she breathed, the words barely audible.

They shifted on the couch, Julia's back finding the cushions as his lips drifted from hers, charting a slow, deliberate path down her jawline to the curve of her neck, lingering at the spot just below her ear. A soft moan escaped her as a delicious ache spread through her.

"I've thought about this for so long," Dylan confessed, his voice low, each word a brushstroke of anticipation.

"So have I," Julia said, her fingers threading through his hair as he continued his tender exploration, kissing along her collarbone, a whisper igniting every nerve ending.

They lost themselves in each other—soft sighs and

breaths, the brush of skin, the slow dance of hands discovering new territory. Each touch was a question, each response an affirmation of the exquisite desire that had been building between them for months, a gentle unfolding of a love they'd both yearned for. When they finally broke apart, hearts still racing, a soft blush high on Julia's cheeks, Dylan's shirt was half-unbuttoned and Julia's hair, a wild, beautiful mess, had completely escaped its pins.

They stayed curled together on the couch for a long time, Julia's head on Dylan's chest, his fingers combing through her hair. The late afternoon light was starting to fade, casting long shadows across the apartment.

Julia would play this moment again and again, later, aching for more of him.

"Dylan?" she said, lifting up from his chest. "There's something I need to tell you."

He tensed slightly. "Oh?"

"I've been offered a job. In Boston." She felt his sharp intake of breath.

Dylan was quiet for a while. "Boston?" he said finally.

"It's a great opportunity. Great firm, challenging projects . . . And we'd be closer."

"Is that why you'd take it?"

Julia considered the question seriously. "I had no idea you were coming. But also because it's the right next step for my career."

Dylan's hand stilled in her hair. "I don't want to be the reason you uproot your life, Julia."

"You wouldn't be. You'd be a signing bonus!" She sat up, facing him. "The question is, what do we do about this? About us?"

"I just want to be near you," Dylan said. "Whatever it takes. If you move to Boston, great. If you stay here, I'll figure out how to make it work. But more importantly," he said, smiling. "What should we do to celebrate? Should we go out to dinner somewhere?"

Julia's eyes glinted, a warm feeling spreading through her. "I have just the thing," she said, standing up.

Julia moved to her kitchen and reached into the refrigerator. When she turned back, she held a bottle of what looked like liquid amber between both hands.

"Is that—?" Dylan's eyes widened, recognizing the distinct shape.

"1967 Château d'Yquem," Julia confirmed, settling back beside him. "From my grandmother's collection. And don't worry," she added with a knowing smile, "it's been on the top shelf, near the front, so it's perfectly cooled, not frozen."

"Dylan stared at the bottle, then at her. "Julia, you can't open that. It's worth thousands of dollars."

"I know," she said, meeting his gaze. "I read something

on Reddit about waiting for the perfect moment."

He smiled. "Yeah. Something about a bag of chips making the occasion special. But what could be more special than this?" he said, looking at her.

Julia grabbed two glasses from her cabinet—not the finest crystal, but clean and clear. Dylan opened the bottle with ceremonial care.

The wine was liquid gold in their glasses, catching the last rays of sunlight streaming through the windows. Julia held hers up.

"To wine threads," she said.

"To meddling neighbors," Dylan added, clinking his glass against hers.

"To mysterious uncles."

"To rare treasures," Dylan said, his eyes never leaving her face.

They sipped the wine and could hardly believe it. It was a liquid symphony of apricot jam, caramelized orange peel, and toasted nuts with deep notes of acacia honey, and a hint of exotic spice. It was everything the legendary vintage promised and so much more. It was as complex as CabernetCrusader had said, a wine that seemed to unfold endlessly on the palate, like the promise of something great.

In the golden light of a Savannah evening, with the taste of wine on their lips and the promise of tomorrow in their hearts, they toasted to the kind of love that was worth every risk, every leap of hope, every perfect imperfect moment that had brought them together.

"I'm glad I didn't cancel our meeting in Boston," Julia said.

"I'm glad you couldn't find my nonexistent website," Dylan replied, tucking a strand of hair behind her ear.

"The universe's most effective filtering system," Julia laughed. "Only the truly persistent make it through."

"Worth the wait," Dylan said, before kissing her again.

For a time in the 16th century, the search for rarer and more beautiful tulips became a passion in Europe. The most elusive of all was the Black Tulip, a symbol of a quest for that which is truly unique.

ABOUT THE AUTHOR

Marisol Murano burns more manuscripts than soufflés—
both tend to collapse under pressure. By day, she's a chef;
by night, she chases swoony words on her keyboard. She
is the best-selling author of *The Lady, The Chef and the
Courtesan*, which won a Romance Writers of America RITA
Award as well as the Original Voices award. Her cat,
Calamity, judges her harshly for the abysmal quality of her
lap, which is prone to sudden, inexplicable movements
when plots are not going her way. Marisol believes that
good romances, like a good sauce, need a steady simmer
and the right amount of spice.